Avi
the Ambulance

Goes to School

Written and illustrated by Claudia Carlson

APPLES & HONEY PRESS

Dedication

To Jacqueline Goldman, whose more than 60 years of dedication and support of
Magen David Adom and whose vision for telling the story of Israel's heroes to new generations
were the inspiration and fuel for creating this book. With our sincerest gratitude.

A special thanks to Donna Fried Calcaterra, Paula Blaine Cohen, Dan Dobin, Barry Feldman, and Mitchel Maidman
for their time, commitment, guidance, good counsel, and most of all, enthusiasm in helping take the idea for
this book and making it a reality. And our thanks and admiration to the more than 14,000 professionals and
volunteers at Magen David Adom, who put the Jewish value of *chai* into action every day by saving lives in Israel.

Additional thanks to Caitlin Allen, Tom Lichtenheld, Bianca Hunter Macnaughton, Erica Carlson Morrell,
Flash Rosenberg, Stephen Roxburgh, Heather Wood, and Paul Zelinsky. — CC

Apples & Honey Press
An imprint of Behrman House
Millburn, New Jersey 07041
www.applesandhoneypress.com

The publisher gratefully acknowledges the following sources of photographs: p. 32: arm in cast © Rudchenko
Liliia/Shutterstock; soccer teammates © Amy Myers/Shutterstock; nurse with child © Monkey Business
Images/Shutterstock; helping hand © Andrey Kuzmin/Shutterstock; Shabbat candles © Noam Armonn/
Shutterstock; fingers in splint © Praisaeng/Shutterstock; volunteers picking up litter © wavebreakmedia/
Shutterstock. All other photos used by permission from Magen David Adom.

Library of Congress Cataloging-in-Publication Data

Carlson, Claudia, author, illustrator.
  Avi the Ambulance Goes to School / written and illustrated by Claudia Carlson.
    pages cm
  Summary: Avi the ambulance, the youngest member of a family of emergency response vehicles,
learns how to zig-and-zag, zoom-and-stop, treat patients well, and drive gently. Includes author's note
on Magen David Adom, Israel's ambulance, blood services, and disaster relief organzation.
  ISBN 978-1-68115-503-6
  [1. Ambulances--Fiction. 2. Emergency vehicles--Fiction. 3. Assistance in emergencies--Fiction.
4. Rescue work--Fiction. 5. Jews--Israel--Fiction. 6. Israel--Fiction.] I. Title.
  PZ7.1.C4Av 2015
  [E]--dc23
                        2014043003

Design by Claudia Carlson • Edited by Ann D. Koffsky and Dena Neusner
Printed in China
1 3 5 7 9 8 6 4 2

0723/B1163/A3

In a garage in Jerusalem lived a family of ambulances.
Some were big. Some were small.
Avi was the youngest and one of the smallest.

3

Avi's family loved to help people.

His big sister, Maya, flashed her lights
and sang, "woooo-woooo-wooo"
as she rushed sick or hurt people to the hospital.

His big brother, Benny, rumbled his engine
and honked, "*toot-toot-toot*"
as he brought blood to hospitals for sick people.

"I want to help, too!" said Avi.
"You're not ready," said Father.
"Avi, you must go to ambulance school to learn to drive safely," said Mother.

"Is it very, very hard?" asked Avi.
"It's hard work, but fun," said Father.

They learned how to zig and zag.

They learned how to zoom and stop.

They learned how to load patients quickly and safely.

Finally, Avi and Zack graduated.

"I'm a lifesaving ambulance now!" said Avi.

"I'm a medic!" said Zack.

Avi's lights flashed as he and Zack got their diplomas.

"Tomorrow I will do good things," thought Avi.
He went to bed and dreamed brave dreams.

In the morning, Zack ate his breakfast
while Avi got a full tank of gas.

First, Maya zoomed to work.
Then Benny left.

But when Avi tried to go, he wobbled.

"Ouch!" yelled Avi.

He bumped to a stop.

"No fair! Heroes aren't supposed to have flat tires!"

"Don't worry. I'll change your tire," said Zack.

"Hurry, hurry," said Avi.

When Zack was done, Avi looked at his reflection in the window.
His new tire felt good and Avi felt ready.

Later, their radio came on.

"Girl hurt, needs help. Avi, you are the nearest and the right size.
"Avi, go...go...go!"

Avi sang, "*woooo-wooo-wooo.*"
He flashed his lights. He roared his engine.

He drove on a narrow street his brother, Benny, was too wide for.
He zoomed under an arch his sister, Maya, was too tall for.

Soon Avi arrived. A girl was sitting by the side of the road.
"What's your name?" asked Zack.

"I'm Shira," she sniffed.
"I fell off my bike. I was riding fast
so I could get home to help
my Ima prepare Shabbat dinner."

"My leg really hurts."

"I know how that feels," said Avi.
"We fixed my tire today.
I will drive you to the hospital."

Zack put a splint on Shira's leg
to keep it still and safe.
Then Zack put her in the back of Avi.

Avi drove gently.

Soon, they arrived at the hospital.

"That was fast!" said Shira.

"It's fun to go fast, but we learned how to do it safely in ambulance school," Avi said proudly.

"That's how we help save lives," added Zack.

"Is ambulance school hard?" asked Shira.

"It was hard work, but fun," said Avi.

Avi and Zack said goodbye to Shira.
Her Abba met Shira and her Ima at the hospital.

When I grow up I want to be like Avi and Zack and help people.

Avi and Zack were tired and happy.
"We're real heroes now," said Zack.
"We're a good team," said Avi.
"See you tomorrow!"

Avi took a bath, scrubbed his grill,
and sipped water to cool his engine.

When Avi returned to the garage, everyone cheered.

"We're proud of you," said his parents.
"Now you're one of us," said Benny.
"You did really well," said Maya.

That night, Avi felt like a hero
for helping someone
on his very first day.

And Avi and Zack made a new friend.

The lifesaving work of MDA

Avi is an ambulance who wants to keep up with his older brothers and sisters. But in order to do so, he must go to paramedic school. The story of Avi is based on the real work of Magen David Adom, Israel's ambulance, blood-services, and disaster-relief organization, serving as emergency medical first responders for the state's more than 8 million people.

Avi the Ambulance Goes to School shows how Jewish values are observed, learned, and applied: *Piku'ach Nefesh*, the importance of saving lives; *Z'rizut*, contributing to society enthusiastically and swiftly; and *Hakarat Hatov*, expressing appreciation to others for their help.

More than 14,000 professionals and volunteers help save lives at MDA. You can learn more at www.afmda.org.

Ambulance

Mobile Intensive Care Unit (MICU)

Bloodmobile

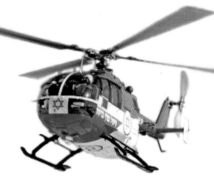

Helicopter

Command Car

Medicycle

Can you match the characters in the story to photos on this page? Hint, look at pages 2 and 3.

Vocabulary

ambulance A special truck used to move hurt or sick people to a hospital, where doctors and nurses take care of them. The ambulance has medical supplies inside. Avi is an ambulance.

bloodmobile A truck where people can give a little of their healthy blood, which can be stored and given to hospitals for sick or hurt people. Benny is a bloodmobile.

cast A hard, strong bandage put around a broken bone, such as a leg or arm, until the bone is healed. A cast was put on Shira's leg.

gurney A small bed on wheels used to move hurt or sick people in and out of ambulances on the way to the hospital. Shira was on a gurney in the back of the ambulance.

hakarat hatov The Jewish value of showing appreciation to others for their help.

hospital A special building where doctors, nurses, and others take care of hurt and sick people.

medic A person trained to help take care of hurt or sick people on the way to the hospital. Zack is a medic.

medicycle A special motorcycle used by Magen David Adom to reach sick and hurt people fast, until an ambulance can get there. Moti is a medicycle.

medical supplies Ambulances and hospitals have medical supplies, such as bandages, splints, gurneys, computers, equipment, and medicine.

MICU (Mobile Intensive Care Unit) A bigger ambulance that has more medical supplies to take care of people who are very hurt or sick. Maya is a MICU.

piku'ach nefesh The Jewish value of saving a life, so important that it supersedes virtually every other commandment.

Shabbat The weekly Jewish day of rest that begins on Friday at sundown.

splint A hard piece of plastic or metal put around a hurt arm, leg, or finger to keep it safe and still until it can be cared for by a doctor. Shira wore a splint in the ambulance.

z'rizut The Jewish value of contributing to society enthusiastically and swiftly.